The Mystery of the Traveling Button

THREE COUSINS DETECTIVE CLUB®

———

9703

The Mystery of the Traveling Button

Elspeth Campbell Murphy
Illustrated by Joe Nordstrom

Bibles & Publications
5706 Monkland Ave.,
Montreal, QC., H4A 1E6   514-481-6335
Orders 800-387-6335 Fax 514-486-9701

BETHANY HOUSE PUBLISHERS
MINNEAPOLIS, MINNESOTA 55438

The Mystery of the Traveling Button
Copyright © 1997
Elspeth Campbell Murphy

Cover and story illustrations by Joe Nordstrom

THREE COUSINS DETECTIVE CLUB® and TCDC® are
registered trademarks of Elspeth Campbell Murphy.

Published by Bethany House Publishers
A Ministry of Bethany Fellowship, Inc.
11300 Hampshire Avenue South
Minneapolis, Minnesota 55438

Printed in the United States of America.

Library of Congress Cataloging-in-Publication Data

Murphy, Elspeth Campbell.   The mystery of the traveling button /
by Elspeth Campbell Murphy.
       p.   cm. — (Three Cousins Detective Club ; #16)
       Summary: The mysterious appearance of a Teddy Roosevelt
campaign button on Tim's baseball cap attracts the attention of an
unscrupulous collector.
       ISBN 1–55661–854–9 (pbk.)
       [1. Collectors and collecting—Fiction. 2. Cousins—Fiction.
3. Mystery and detective stories.] I. Title. II. Series: Murphy,
Elspeth Campbell. Three Cousins Detective Club ; 16.
PZ7.M95316Mykt   1997
[Fic]—dc21   97–21122
                                                                CIP
                                                                 AC

ELSPETH CAMPBELL MURPHY has been a familiar name in Christian publishing for over fifteen years, with more than seventy-five books to her credit and sales reaching five million worldwide. She is the author of the best-selling series *David and I Talk to God* and *The Kids From Apple Street Church*, as well as the 1990 Gold Medallion winner *Do You See Me, God?* A graduate of Trinity College and Moody Bible Institute, Elspeth and her husband, Mike, make their home in Chicago, where she writes full time.

Contents

"Wealth you get by dishonesty will do you no good, but honesty can save your life."

Proverbs 10:2

1

Feeling Fine

*T*he funny little green car was back again today.

Timothy Dawson noticed it in the way that he noticed everything. But he didn't think too much about it. He had other things on his mind.

Bright and early he had gotten himself a bowl of cereal and come out on the front porch to eat it.

He felt fine.

The night before, he had sung a solo at the retirement dinner for his father's boss. Timothy had been really worried about the solo, but everything had gone great.

It was a funny thing about time, Timothy thought to himself. You could have something hard ahead of you. And you could wonder how you were ever going to get through it. Then suddenly—it's behind you. You got through it. You're on the other side. And you don't even have to think about it anymore if you don't want to.

But Timothy was enjoying thinking about it. He had done his best on something hard. A good feeling!

Timothy also felt fine because his cousins Sarah-Jane Cooper and Titus McKay were still at his house. They had come along with him to the dinner last night. A good thing, too. Otherwise Timothy would have been the only kid there.

The little green car drove by slowly again until it turned the corner and was out of sight.

Timothy paid more attention to the car this time. It didn't belong to anyone on his block that he knew. He hadn't seen it on his street until—when? Yesterday. He had been playing outside with his cousins. Titus had pointed it out because it was so unusual looking. And Timothy had remembered seeing it before—where? Early yesterday morning at a garage sale on the next block.

Timothy, up bright and early, had gone over to help. If anyone got up earlier than Timothy, it was people who came to garage sales! Mr. and Mrs. Simmons were friends of Timothy's family. And Timothy had played with their grandson, who was visiting. Everyone joked about how much the boys looked alike even though they weren't related. Todd was younger and shorter than Timothy, but they both had blond hair, bleached even blonder by the sun.

Then it had been time for Timothy to come home and play with his real relatives. Busy day!

Timothy looked up quickly. He thought he caught a glimpse of the car again. But he couldn't be sure. He told himself he might be making too much of it just because he liked mysteries.

Titus and Sarah-Jane liked mysteries, too. In fact, the three cousins even had a detective club. A good thing, too. At the retirement dinner, they had been able to solve a tricky little mystery for his father's boss.

Timothy figured Sarah-Jane would be up before too long.

Titus was another story altogether.

11

Titus was *never* bright-eyed and bushy-tailed first thing in the morning. Timothy decided to let him sleep a little longer. Later he would send his sister, Priscilla, in to play for Titus on her little drum.

A-rum-pa-pa-pum.

Actually, it was more like *BANG! BANG! BANG!* Priscilla was just a toddler. And "The Little Drummer Boy" she wasn't. But she was loud. You had to give her that.

Suddenly Timothy was aware that the house was quiet. Too quiet. Priscilla should have been up and about, making noise by now.

This was not good.

The only time she was this quiet was when she was sound asleep—or getting into his stuff.

Timothy kept his stuff up high. But lately Priscilla had learned to climb.

So much for feeling fine.

With a sigh, Timothy got up and went to investigate.

2

The Quiet Toddler

*T*imothy was good at investigation. So how hard could it be to solve The Mystery of the Quiet Toddler?

As it turned out, not hard at all.

The door to his room stood open.

Timothy was sure he had closed it.

He crept closer and listened.

He heard a soft *Clink! Clink! Clink!* and Priscilla talking to herself.

"No, no! Mustn't dood it!" *Clink!* "Sibby's buddons? No! Timmy's buddons." *Clink!* "Sibby get owie fwum buddons." *Clink!* "Mustn't dood it!" *Clink!*

Before he even saw her, Timothy realized what Priscilla was doing. With a yowl he rushed into the room.

13

Priscilla looked up guiltily.

"MOM!" wailed Timothy.

Timothy's mother came running. She was followed closely by Sarah-Jane.

From the look on his mother's face, Timothy could tell she thought someone had died. "What!? What is it? What happened?" she cried.

"My baseball cap!" wailed Timothy.

All the time Priscilla had been telling herself not to, she had been pulling the metal buttons off Timothy's baseball cap and dropping them in a little pile on the floor.

Timothy's mother clapped a hand to her chest. "For goodness' sake, Timothy! You just about gave me heart failure."

"Well, she knows she's not supposed to get into my button collection!" said Timothy. "And I put my baseball cap up high just like you said. But she climbed up there and got it anyway."

Timothy pointed at the bedpost on the top bunk.

On the top bunk, Titus sat up slowly and blinked sleepily. "Did someone just say something?" he asked.

"Remind me not to hire you as a night watchman, Ti!" Timothy told him. "You'd let anyone in."

"OK," said Titus. He blinked again. "What?"

"Priscilla got in and messed with Tim's stuff," Sarah-Jane explained.

"Oh," said Titus. "OK."

Timothy's mother picked Priscilla up and spoke firmly to her. "Are these Priscilla's buttons? No. These are Timothy's buttons. Priscilla will get an owie from buttons. They're too sharp for her! Priscilla must not touch them."

Priscilla nodded solemnly. "Mustn't dood it."

"That's right!" said Timothy's mother, sounding very pleased. "Good girl. You're learning, aren't you?"

"Ha," said Timothy.

Mrs. Dawson took Priscilla downstairs while Timothy, Titus, and Sarah-Jane surveyed the damage.

3

The Baseball Cap

*I*t was nothing that couldn't be fixed. But it was annoying just the same.

Timothy was very fussy about his baseball cap. Sometimes he wore it completely plain. But other times he wore it with metal buttons pinned all over it.

Timothy had a large collection of metal buttons. Big buttons, little buttons. New buttons, old buttons.

Some of the buttons were advertising something. Some of them were for sports teams. Some of them were souvenirs of places Timothy had been. And some of the buttons had the names and even pictures of people who had run for president.

Timothy had more buttons in his collection than he could wear at any one time. That meant he had to rotate them.

But that was OK. Timothy loved art. He loved the buttons for their colors and designs and the perfectly round shape of them. He loved arranging the buttons in interesting patterns.

Whenever it was time to rotate the buttons, Timothy would begin by taking all the buttons off the cap and putting them in a pile. Priscilla had watched him do this only a couple of days ago.

Unfortunately.

The annoying part was that he had gotten the buttons *exactly* the way he wanted them. He hadn't been planning on working on his cap for a while.

Timothy sighed. Maybe if he spread the buttons out on the floor, he could remember how he had them.

Titus and Sarah-Jane helped him turn them over.

Suddenly Timothy said, "That's funny!"

"Funny ha-ha? Or funny weird?" asked Titus, who was pretty much awake by now.

"Funny *weird*!" said Timothy.

"What's funny weird?" asked Sarah-Jane.

"This button," said Timothy, holding it up for his cousins to see.

"What about it?" asked Sarah-Jane. "It's a really nice one."

"It's a great-looking button," said Titus.

"Yes, it *is* a great button," agreed Timothy. "The weird part is that it isn't mine."

4

The Mysterious Button

*H*is cousins stared at him.

"What do you mean it's not yours?" asked Titus. "Priscilla just pulled it off your cap."

"I know she did," said Timothy. "But I also know that I have never seen this button before in my life."

"Then, how did the button get on your cap?" asked Titus.

"I don't know," replied Timothy. "All I know is that it wasn't there when I put the other buttons on my cap a couple of days ago."

They sat in silence for a moment, as if none of them could think of what to say about the situation.

Finally Sarah-Jane said, "I think you should be grateful to Priscilla."

"What!" exclaimed Timothy. "Why?" Sometimes it amazed him how much girl cousins stuck together.

"Because," said Sarah-Jane, "if she hadn't pulled all the buttons off your cap, you wouldn't have noticed the new button."

"I would have noticed it eventually," said Timothy. "It's pretty big. And I *love* the picture on it. It's neat-O!"

"It's EX-cellent!" agreed Titus.

"So cool!" said Sarah-Jane.

Sarah-Jane had called the button "new." And it *was* new—to Timothy. But actually, it was very old.

On the button there was a picture and some words. The picture showed a man on a horse. The man wore a big hat and unusual-looking glasses. He had a big mustache. The words around the top of the button said: *Theodore Roosevelt for President 1904.*

Even though the button was old, it was in excellent condition—as if someone had been taking very good care of it.

"It's the best button in my whole collection," said Timothy.

He stopped and thought about that for a

minute. Yes, the button had gotten into his collection. Who knew how? But did that mean it was his to keep?

He told his cousins what he was thinking.

"Well," said Sarah-Jane, sounding a little doubtful about what she was going to say. "Maybe someone meant to give you a little present but didn't want you to know who it was from. You know—like a 'secret pal' or something."

"Yes," said Titus. "What is it they say? Someone 'wished to remain anonymous.'"

"Maybe . . ." said Timothy slowly. "But I can't help thinking there must be some mistake."

Much as he loved the button, Timothy knew he had to at least try to find out where it came from. If it was a mistake, then the owner needed to get the button back. And if it was a 'secret pal'? Well, Timothy was so curious about things, he knew that would drive him crazy until he found out who it was.

Again Timothy told his cousins what he was thinking. And from the way they nodded, he could tell they were thinking the same thing. The mystery of the button needed solving.

And they were just the people to do it.

5

An Important Phone Call

*T*he first step in solving the mystery was to get dressed. Titus and Sarah-Jane were still in their bathrobes. Sarah-Jane went off to the nursery she shared with Priscilla when she visited. While Titus got dressed in Timothy's room, Timothy pinned the buttons back on his cap.

He was really tempted to pin the "new" button with the others. But he didn't want anything to happen to it. So he carefully wrapped it in a clean handkerchief. The second step in solving the mystery would be showing the button to his mother.

The cousins met at the top of the stairs and

went down to breakfast. (Titus and Sarah-Jane's first. Timothy's second.)

Timothy showed the button to his mother. His mother was just as puzzled as he was. That was something Timothy was learning about grown-ups. You couldn't expect them to have all the answers instantly just because they were grown-up. Adults needed time to think about things, too.

But Timothy's mother had a good suggestion. She suggested that Titus ask his father about the button. This made sense because Titus's father taught history. He might know something about where such an old, old button might have come from.

Titus's father was coming to pick him up later. But the cousins couldn't wait that long. Titus got on the phone.

When he got off the phone, he had an excited look on his face.

"Well?" cried Timothy and Sarah-Jane together. "What did Uncle Richard say?"

"He said lots of people are collecting political buttons these days. There are whole conventions where people go to buy and sell buttons. And they look at antique stores and

24

flea markets. Anyway, he said Teddy Roosevelt buttons are especially popular because he was such a character. He knows someone who paid fifty dollars for a Teddy Roosevelt button not too long ago."

"Fifty dollars!" exclaimed Sarah-Jane. "For a little metal button?!"

"Yeah, well, it all depends," said Titus. "It depends on how rare the button is and what kind of condition it's in. I described Tim's, but my dad says he doesn't know enough about buttons to guess what it's worth. He's going to call around and get back to us.

"In the meantime, he said we should put the button in a safe place."

"Exactly what I was thinking," said Timothy.

Timothy was good at hiding things.

He took the button that he had wrapped in the handkerchief. And he put the wrapped button in a little plastic sandwich bag.

Then he buried the bag in a box of cereal that nobody in the family liked all that much.

Finally, he got out the kitchen stool and moved the cereal box to a higher shelf.

And all the time Timothy was doing this, he had the feeling he was being watched.

6

Questions

*T*imothy couldn't understand where the feeling of being watched was coming from.

His cousins were watching him. But it wasn't that.

His mother was watching him, too. But it wasn't that, either.

And, of course, Priscilla was watching him.

Priscilla was *always* watching him. Always trying to copy him. Right now she was positively fascinated.

But not even this explained the peculiar feeling. Timothy told himself that he was just jumpy because of the whole odd button situation.

"Buddon in dere!" said Priscilla, pointing

a chubby little finger as Timothy closed the cupboard door.

"Don't even *think* about it!" Timothy told her sternly.

"Mustn't dood it," replied Priscilla—the very picture of innocence.

"Yeah, right," muttered Timothy. "I've heard *that* song and dance before."

Timothy put the stool away.

Then he and his cousins wandered outside. They were all feeling kind of restless.

"*Now* what do we do?" Timothy asked.

Sarah-Jane shrugged. "Wait for Uncle Richard to call back, I guess."

"Yes," said Titus. "But even if my dad finds out more about the button, it still won't tell us how it got on Tim's cap."

Sarah-Jane nodded. "The question is: *Who?* Who's going to come up and pin a fifty-dollar button on some kid's cap? And: *Why?*"

Titus said, "Maybe whoever gave the button to Tim didn't know it might be worth fifty dollars. And of course, it might *not* be. My dad said it all depends on how rare it is."

Timothy said, "Expensive or not, what I'd like to know is: *How?* How did someone pin the button on the cap without me knowing it?"

"Maybe you weren't wearing it at the time," said Sarah-Jane. "Maybe it happened when the cap wasn't on your head. That's another question: *When?* When did it happen? You said the button wasn't on your cap when you pinned the buttons on a couple days ago. So it must have happened sometime between then and now."

"Good thinking, S-J," said Timothy. "So all I have to do now is think about: *Where?* Where was I recently?"

7

Thinking Back

*T*itus said, "Well, last night we were at the retirement dinner. And you definitely weren't wearing your cap then. You wanted to, but it was a dress-up thing, so your parents made you leave your cap at home. You put it on the bedpost of the top bunk, where you thought Priscilla couldn't get it."

"Ha!" said Timothy. "That kid is into everything. But you're right, Ti. The cap was off my head from when we got dressed for the dinner until this morning when Priscilla got her grubby little paws on it."

"That's not a very nice thing to say about your baby sister," Sarah-Jane told him. "Although, I have to admit, sometimes when I pick her up, she *is* a little sticky."

Titus said, "Hey, what about the baby-sitter? She was home alone with Priscilla last night. She could have put the button on your cap."

Timothy groaned.

"What's wrong?" his cousins asked him.

Timothy said, "The baby-sitter is this snotty teenager who loves baby girls but who thinks boys our age are all crazy. I really hate to ask her."

But in the end, not knowing was worse than asking. Timothy made the call.

"What did she say?" asked Titus.

"She said I was crazy," replied Timothy. "And I think we can cross her off the list of people who would leave me little presents. So—moving right along . . ."

"All right," said Sarah-Jane. "Let's think back. You didn't wear your cap to the retirement dinner. But you did wear it before we got ready to go. You were wearing it the whole time we were playing outside yesterday afternoon."

"Yes," said Titus. "But you weren't home when we first got here. So we sat on the steps and waited for you. It was only a couple of minutes. Then we saw you coming. And you were definitely wearing your cap then. And there was this odd-looking green car. And you laughed and said maybe it was following you because you had just seen it—at your neighbor's garage sale! *That's* where you were before you came home to meet up with us. You were at a garage sale! My dad said people look for buttons at flea markets. And a garage sale is sort of like a little flea market."

"Did they have buttons at the garage sale?" asked Sarah-Jane.

"Not any I saw," replied Timothy. "But I *do* remember that I took my cap off."

8

Squashed Petunias

*T*imothy said, "I think I remember taking my cap off and putting it on a lawn chair while I was working. Mr. Simmons might know something about it."

At least going to talk to his neighbor gave them something to do while they were waiting for Uncle Richard to call back.

The cousins went in to tell Timothy's mother where they were going. On the way inside, Timothy noticed something.

The petunias under the kitchen window were squashed.

He pointed this out to Sarah-Jane and Titus and said, "Looks like Priscilla is up to her old tricks. Last week she pulled the heads off a neighbor's marigolds. If my mom looks

away for even a couple of seconds, Priscilla
gets into stuff. Anyway, my mom made the
neighbors a batch of her special cookies to
apologize."

"Well, at least she didn't pull the heads off
the petunias," said Titus. "They're just
squashed down a little. Maybe we can prop
them up when we get back."

"We definitely shouldn't tell on her,"
Sarah-Jane said firmly. "It sounds like she's in
enough trouble already."

As they went upstairs they could hear Priscilla shouting, "No no no no no no no!"

"Her favorite word," explained Timothy. "Probably Mom is just trying to get her dressed or something."

"Hey, Sib, come here!" Timothy called to her. There was something he had to find out.

When she came running, he knelt down and said, "Now, listen. Here's the deal. You be a good girl for Mommy, and we won't tell her how you squashed her flowers."

Priscilla stared at him blankly. Usually when she'd been up to something, you could tell by the guilty look on her face. But now she just looked puzzled.

Timothy sighed. "OK, Sib. Be a good girl and get dressed, and we'll take you with us."

It worked like a charm. There was nothing Priscilla liked better than tagging along with Timothy.

Timothy's mother was delighted, too. She had a lot of work to do, and it was easier without Priscilla.

Sarah-Jane put her little girl cousin in the stroller, and the four of them headed off.

On the way out, Timothy showed Priscilla the squashed petunias.

Priscilla shook her head so hard he thought it would fall off.

"Sibby. Fwowers. No no dood it!"

Timothy didn't know how the flowers had gotten squashed. But he knew one thing for sure. Priscilla hadn't done it.

9

Teddy Roosevelt

"*T*here's that green car again," remarked Titus.

Timothy looked up in time to see it speed by and turn the corner at the end of the block.

"Maybe he's driving around looking for another garage sale," suggested Sarah-Jane. "Some people do that, you know."

"Could be," said Timothy. But the green car just seemed to him to be one more odd thing in a day full of odd things. A funny-looking green car. A mysterious button. The feeling of being watched. Squashed petunias. What next?

The day got even odder when he explained to Mr. Simmons about the button.

Mr. Simmons burst out laughing and

clapped Timothy on the shoulder. "Well, of course!" he exclaimed. "Old Charlie's back in town!"

"Ex-*cuse* me?" said Timothy.

Mr. Simmons sat them down and explained.

"My old friend Charlie Green and I have been playing this joke on each other for years and years.

"It started way back when Charlie and I were roommates in college. I had stayed up all night studying for a history test on President Theodore Roosevelt. Well, I did fine on the test. And that afternoon there was a contest on the radio. The third caller with the correct answer would win a prize. I don't remember the question. But I knew the answer was 'Teddy Roosevelt.'

"Well, I was just so excited because I thought I knew everything there was to know on *that* subject! But when my call went through, I drew a complete blank. I was so tired from being up all night I couldn't even remember my *own* name. I just stood there saying, 'Um . . . um . . .' until the announcer said my time was up.

"Well, Charlie never said anything. But a couple of days later, I was sitting in class, and I realized something was scratching at my neck. Something pinned to the collar of my shirt. When I pulled it out, I saw it was a metal button that said, '*Theodore Roosevelt for President.*'

"I knew it had to be Charlie. He loved to shop for odd little things in junk stores. But I never said anything. I waited until we were packing for vacation. Then I hid the button in his hairbrush.

"Ever since then, that button has traveled back and forth between us. Always showing up in the most unusual places. And neither of us ever says a word about it. I don't know what we'd do if we ever lost it. We both take good care of it when it's our turn to have it."

Timothy had a sudden thought. "I bet your friend Charlie saw me helping at your garage sale and thought I must be your grandson Todd. He figured sooner or later you would notice the button on 'Todd's' cap."

"Well, now! I imagine you're right about that, Timothy!" said Mr. Simmons. "Charlie knew I was having a garage sale. He must have snuck over here and pinned the button on your cap when it was lying on the lawn chair.

"I remember seeing your cap because someone actually tried to buy it! The guy got quite huffy when Mrs. Simmons explained that it was your private property."

Timothy said slowly, "I don't suppose your friend Charlie *Green* drives a *green* car, does he?"

Mr. Simmons looked at him in surprise. "No, he doesn't. But you know who does— that guy who tried to buy your cap."

10

The T.C.Ð.C.

*I*n Timothy's opinion, the sooner the button was safely back with Mr. Simmons, the better. He suggested that Mr. Simmons come home with them to get it.

On the way back, Titus told Mr. Simmons that the button might be worth fifty dollars. Mr. Simmons was surprised.

Sarah-Jane told him about Timothy's hiding place for the button. Mr. Simmons was impressed.

"It's really something how you kids thought all this through!" he said.

"You can depend on the T.C.D.C.," said Titus.

"What's a 'teesy-deesy'?" asked Mr. Simmons.

"It's letters," explained Sarah-Jane. "Capital T. Capital C. Capital D. Capital C. It stands for the Three Cousins Detective Club."

"Detectives, eh? Well, it certainly sounds as if you know what you're doing."

When they came into the kitchen, Timothy called upstairs to his mother, "Mom! We're home!"

As his mother came in, Priscilla pointed to the cupboard and said to Mr. Simmons, "Buddon in dere!"

But before Timothy could climb up to get it, the phone rang.

Titus answered, guessing that it might be his father. He was right.

Timothy heard him say, "What do you mean 'am I sitting down?'?"

Then suddenly Titus sat down with a thud and handed the phone to Mr. Simmons.

Timothy and Sarah-Jane rushed over to Titus. "Well? Well? What did your dad have to say?" they asked together.

Titus gulped. "He said a button like that one recently sold for more than a thousand dollars."

Timothy and Sarah-Jane gulped and sat down with a thud.

"Wow!" said Timothy's mother. "Who would have guessed it?"

"Not me, certainly," said Mr. Simmons, joining them at the table. "Titus's father tells me collecting political buttons has become a hot hobby. Collectors of anything can get a little crazy when it comes to their collections. They'll sometimes do just about anything to get their hands on something they need to make their collections complete. He said the highest anyone's paid for a button so far is fifty thousand dollars."

Timothy thought you could practically hear all their jaws dropping open.

"I must say," continued Mr. Simmons. "This takes some of the fun out of the little game Charlie and I have been playing all these years. It's one thing to send a funny little button traveling all around. It's another thing when you know that funny little button is a rare antique worth big bucks. It's always meant a lot to us personally, of course. But we never knew all these collectors would love to get hold of it!"

"Buddon in dere!" said Priscilla, pointing at the cupboard.

"Oh! Right!" exclaimed Timothy. "I almost forgot!"

Everyone laughed a little nervously. They were still trying to get used to the news about the button.

Timothy climbed up to get the cereal box. He was glad—now more than ever!—that he had picked such a good hiding place.

He put the cereal box in the center of the table. He pulled out the plastic sandwich bag. He carefully unwrapped his handkerchief.

The button was gone.

11

Missing

*F*or several long moments they all just stared at the empty handkerchief. It was as if they thought by staring hard enough they could make the button suddenly appear. No one could think of a thing to say.

Except Priscilla.

She pointed at the empty handkerchief and asked innocently, "Buddon go bye-bye?"

Timothy's first thought was that Priscilla had somehow gotten up to the high cupboard. But he ruled it out right away.

In the first place, even if she had been able to climb that high, she couldn't have done the rest. Unpack the cereal box. Take out the button. Refold the handkerchief so neatly. Priscilla never did anything neatly.

And in the second place, she had an iron-clad alibi for the whole time. She had either been upstairs with their mother or at Mr. Simmons' house with her brother and cousins.

At no time had Priscilla been alone in the kitchen.

So who had?

His mother? But she wouldn't have moved the button without telling him.

All this flitted through Timothy's mind faster than he could say it.

Titus said, "What happened to it? How

could the button be gone? It might be a traveling button, but it couldn't just get up and walk away."

"A burglar?" said Sarah-Jane. "Did a burglar break in and steal it?"

"A burglar wouldn't have to break in," said Timothy. "In the summertime we're always going in and out. So the screen door isn't locked."

"I was upstairs the whole time you kids were gone," said Timothy's mother with a worried frown. "But it doesn't look as if anything has been touched in here. Nothing is missing except the button. And it was hidden so well. Are we saying someone just walked in here and knew exactly where to look? How could that be? We were the only ones who knew where it was."

"Were we?" said Timothy, more to himself than to the others. A couple of things that had been bothering him suddenly came together and made sense.

12

Checking It Out

*T*imothy led everyone out to the yard. He had a hunch about something, and he needed to check it out. He brought the kitchen step stool with him.

"My petunias!" cried Timothy's mother when she saw the squashed flowers. "What happened to my petunias?" She couldn't help looking at Priscilla.

"Sibby. Fwowers. No!" said Priscilla indignantly.

"It wasn't Priscilla this time," agreed Timothy.

"Then, who?" asked his mother.

"That, I don't know," said Timothy. "But this morning when I was hiding the button, I had the strangest feeling that I was being watched. I didn't say anything because I thought I was imagining things. Now I don't think so."

Timothy set the kitchen step stool on the grass. (He was careful not to do any more damage to the petunias.) He climbed up—but not all the way to the top. He just went up high enough to be about the height of the average grown-up.

"Aha!" cried Timothy. "It's just as I thought."

"What? What?" cried everyone else.

"The petunias are squashed in just that one spot," said Timothy. "Nowhere else. That's because those petunias are under the kitchen window. The window is high. But not too high for a grown-up to stand there and see in. And when you look through the window, you have a perfect view of the cupboard where I hid the button."

"Well, I'll be!" exclaimed Mr. Simmons. "So you do!"

Naturally Sarah-Jane and Titus had to check out the view from the step stool for themselves. So did Priscilla—although she had no idea what she was supposed to be looking at.

"Let me get this straight, Timothy," said his mother. "Are you saying someone took the button because he happened to see you when he was peeking in the window?"

"No," said Timothy. "Just the opposite. I'm saying he was peeking in the window because he knew I had the button."

13

Button, Button

"*T*he man from the garage sale!" cried Sarah-Jane. "The man who tried to buy your baseball cap!"

"The man in the green car!" cried Titus.

"That's what *I* think," said Timothy. "Although I can't *prove* any of it. But here's what I think happened:

"I think the man in the green car came to the garage sale yesterday, looking for buttons. I think he's a collector. And that's what collectors do. I've done it myself.

"Mr. Simmons didn't have any buttons. But I was there helping. And I was wearing a baseball cap that was covered in buttons.

"We didn't know it, but Mr. Simmons' friend Charlie Green was at the garage sale, too. He wasn't there to buy anything. He was looking for a cute place to leave the Theodore Roosevelt button where Mr. Simmons would find it—eventually. Mr. Green saw me helping and thought I was Mr. Simmons' grandson, Todd.

"So when Mr. Green saw my cap on the lawn chair, he snuck up and pinned the button to it, then snuck away.

"I don't know if the man in the green car saw him do this. But I *do* think he spotted the Roosevelt button. And he knew a good thing when he saw it. He offered to buy my whole cap so that he could get the button."

Mr. Simmons said, "And I'm willing to bet he offered a lot less than a thousand dollars for it! But Mrs. Simmons told him he couldn't buy it because the cap was yours. And it was definitely *not for sale!*"

Titus said, "So he followed you home. You joked about that, remember? But it turned out he really was."

"Following my cap, anyway," said Timothy. "I think he's been driving around again today, trying to get his hands on that button. Probably he can't afford a thousand dollars to buy one—even if he could find it. Finally, he tried peeking in the window. He saw where I hid it. And, when the coast was clear, he snuck in here and got it."

Sarah-Jane said, "You'd think a burglar would know better than to drive such a noticeable car."

"I don't think he's a regular burglar, exactly," said Timothy. "I think he's just a collector who's gotten a little nuts about wanting a rare button."

"Ha!" said Sarah-Jane. "There's been stuff I wanted so much I thought I couldn't stand it. But that doesn't mean I snuck into people's kitchens and went through their cereal."

"Speaking of cereal," said Titus. "I assume he didn't take the whole box because we'd notice right away if *that* was gone. He had no way of knowing we'd be opening the box so soon to take the button out."

Mr. Simmons said, "You kids are amazing the way you figured all this out. I agree with you. I think it happened just like you said. Did you ever play that old game? 'Button, Button, Who's Got the Button?' "

"Buddon go bye-bye?" asked Priscilla.

Mr. Simmons smiled sadly at her. "I'm afraid so, sweetheart. My traveling button went bye-bye. And I don't think I'll ever see it again."

Timothy, Titus, and Sarah-Jane looked at one another. Yes, they had done some good detective work, but they didn't feel all that great about it.

The traveling button was gone. And they had no idea how to find it.

But as it turned out, the traveling button found them.

14

Big Brown Box

Timothy, Titus, and Sarah-Jane never thought they would see the green car again.

But they did. Or rather, they caught a glimpse of it.

Mr. and Mrs. Simmons had taken everyone out for hamburgers. And on the way back, they all saw a flash of green heading away from Timothy's street. It was too far away to follow it. In fact, there was some disagreement as to whether or not it was *the* green car.

But when they all got back to Timothy's house, there was a surprise waiting for them on the front porch that kind of settled it.

It was a big brown box. Inside there were four tissue-wrapped bundles and an envelope.

Inside the envelope there was a letter. And something small wrapped up in a small cloth. Carefully Timothy unwrapped it.

It was the Theodore Roosevelt button.

The letter said simply:

Dear Baseball-Cap-Boy,

    I'm sorry I took your button. It is a wonderful piece, worth a great deal of money. I suggest you get an expert to look at it for you. I just know I could never keep it—knowing the crazy thing I did to get hold of it. It was very wrong of me. I need to take a long, hard look at myself! Anyway, I hope you will accept my apology. I also hope you and your two friends and the baby will accept these gifts in honor of our friend, President Theodore Roosevelt.

The letter was not signed. But the "baseball-cap-boy" felt certain it was from the "green-car-man."

The cousins practically dove into the box and tore the tissue paper off the bundles.

The bundles were teddy bears. Beautiful, brand-new teddy bears. Two with bright blue ribbons. Two with pink.

Mr. Simmons laughed in delight. "Teddy bears! How absolutely perfect!"

"Why?" asked Timothy.

"Because teddy bears are named after Theodore Roosevelt," Mr. Simmons explained. " 'Teddy' is a nickname for Theodore. Now, President Roosevelt was known as a big game hunter. Very brave. Well, one day he was on a trip out west, hunting big, ferocious bears. The only problem was, he didn't see any. Only a little cub. Well, of course he let it go. People loved hearing about that. The story spread. There was a woman who made toy bears. And her husband asked the president for permission to call them 'teddy bears.' And so they have been called that ever since."

"I'm not actually going to *play* with mine," said Timothy. "I'm going to put it on a shelf and keep it nice—as a kind of souvenir." He looked right at Priscilla. "A *high* shelf. Where a certain Little Somebody can't get her grubby little paws on it."

Priscilla didn't answer. She was too busy hugging her teddy bear and babbling secrets in his ear.

Timothy knew that from time to time—when no one was looking—he would get his bear down and give it a big hug. He might even tell it a secret or two.

15

The Tie

*T*he phone rang. It was Titus's father saying a collector wanted to come out and see the button if Mr. Simmons wanted to sell it. Mr. Simmons called his friend Mr. Green, and they agreed to meet with the buyer and to sell the traveling button.

"Wow!" said Timothy. "What are you going to do with all that money?"

"Timothy!" cried his mother, looking shocked.

Timothy knew it wasn't polite to ask personal questions like that. But Mr. and Mrs. Simmons just laughed. "It's all right," said Mr. Simmons. "Charlie and I talked it over. And we know *exactly* what we want to do with all that money. Actually, it was the guy in the green car who gave us the idea. We're going to spend every last penny on teddy bears. It's not too soon to be thinking about Christmas toys for needy children. Charlie feels—and I agree with him!—that no child should be without a teddy bear."

While they waited for the buyer, Mr. Simmons took the cousins with him to make photocopies of the button to keep as souvenirs. They made one for Mr. Simmons, one for Mr. Green, and one each for Timothy, Titus, and Sarah-Jane, and one for Priscilla that Timothy would keep for her until she got older.

Sarah-Jane said, "What are you and Mr. Green going to do about the button game now, Mr. Simmons? Are you going to pass the picture back and forth?"

"Well, I suppose we could," said Mr. Simmons a little sadly. "But it wouldn't be the same, would it?"

When they got home, Mr. Green was waiting for them. When Mr. Simmons wasn't looking, Mr. Green pulled the cousins aside.

"Can you keep a secret?" he asked. "On the way over here, I stopped and got a little present for John. I'm not going to hand it to him. I'm going to leave it at his house as a little surprise. But I wanted to get your opinion first."

He opened a box and showed them the ugliest tie the cousins had ever seen. They had been taught that if you can't say something nice, it's better not to say anything at all. So they just stood there staring at it.

"Please!" said Mr. Green. "Say something. Please tell me it's the most hideous tie in the world!"

The cousins burst out laughing.

"It's hideous beyond belief!" said Titus.

"Ghastly!" agreed Sarah-Jane.

Timothy said, "You know—if you give that tie to Mr. Simmons, he's just going to find a way to give it back to you."

Mr. Green winked at them. "I hope so!" he said. "I certainly hope so!"

The End